For my parents

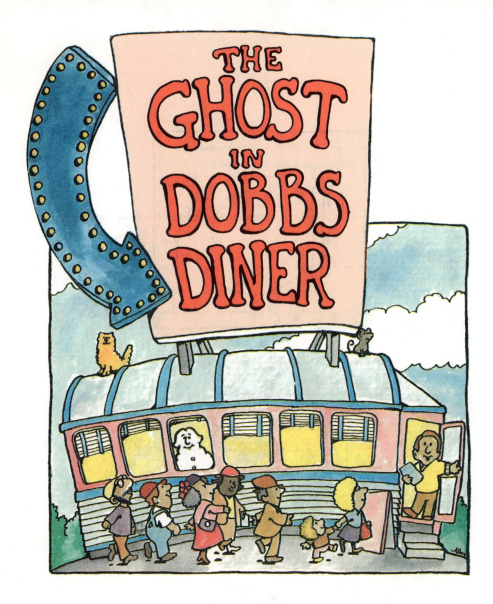

THE GHOST IN DOBBS DINER

by ROBERT ALLEY

Parents Magazine Press • New York

A Parents Magazine
Read Aloud Original

Library of Congress Cataloging in Publication Data.
Alley, Robert. 1955–   The ghost in Dobbs diner.
SUMMARY: The ghost that pops out of the old green
bottle Mr. Dobbs finds is very helpful in the diner,
but the rest of the help and customers are too
frightened to find out what a nice ghost he really is.
[1. Ghost stories. 2. Restaurants, lunch rooms, etc. — Fiction.]
I. Title.   PZ7.A4394Gh   [E]   81-4864
ISBN 0-8193-1055-7   AACR2   ISBN 0-8193-1056-5 (lib. bdg.)

Mr. Dobbs ran the diner
on the corner by the highway.
It was always very busy.

Mr. Dobbs worked so hard that
he never had time to sit down.

He had to help the busboy.

He had to help
the waitress.

He had to help
the cook.

One day, right in the middle of lunch,
the cook ran out of pickles.
"Fiddlesticks!" said the cook.
And he asked Mr. Dobbs for more.

Way in the back of the closet,

Mr. Dobbs found an old, dusty green bottle.

He thought it was a pickle jar.

He unscrewed the top.

Out swirled a twisty, twirly cloud
of white smoke.
It fluttered around for a minute,
then introduced itself.

"Samuel Sheets, ghost and world traveler,"
it said. "Pleased to meet you."
"Oh, my!" was all Mr. Dobbs could say.

When Samuel Sheets saw he was
in Dobbs Diner, he was very happy.
He had always wanted to work in a diner.
He got started right away.
He mopped the floors for the busboy.

He helped the waitress

with her heavy trays.

He even helped the cook with his soup.

Soon everyone in Dobbs Diner was hiding.
"We're not working in a diner with a ghost!"
shouted the busboy, the waitress, and the cook.
"Bottle him up again!"

Mr. Dobbs would not do that.
He liked Samuel Sheets.
"Once you get to know him,
you'll like him, too.

He can even cook," said Mr. Dobbs.

But no one listened.

"We quit!" they shouted.

Samuel Sheets was very hurt.

He wanted to pop himself back into his bottle.

"Don't be silly. We have to make supper,"
said Mr. Dobbs.

And he shooed Samuel Sheets into the kitchen.

But when supper was ready,
no one came.

The busboy, the waitress, and the cook
had run straight to the Mayor.
They had told him about the ghost
in Dobbs Diner.

The Mayor was very upset.

"I will call the police!" he said.

"We must get rid of that thing!"

Mr. Dobbs was about to lock up for the night,
when the Mayor and three police officers
charged through the door.

"Where's that terrible, creepy ghost?"
shouted the Mayor.

Mr. Dobbs tried to explain that
the ghost was not terrible or creepy.
But, again, no one listened.
Things looked bad for Samuel Sheets.

Then Mr. Dobbs had an idea.

He knew that the Mayor loved good food.

So he offered the Mayor the supper
that Samuel Sheets had cooked.
But he didn't tell the Mayor who the cook was.

The Mayor ate everything on his plate.
"That was the best meal I ever had,"
he said happily.
"I must meet the cook."

Mr. Dobbs was happy to
bring in his new helper.

"OH!" cried the Mayor.

And just as Mr. Dobbs had hoped,
the Mayor could not bring himself
to bottle up such a good cook.
Instead, he made friends with Samuel Sheets.

Soon, Dobbs Diner was busier than ever.
The busboy, the waitress, and the cook
found out that working with a ghost
could be a lot of fun.

And Mr. Dobbs finally had time to sit down.

ABOUT THE AUTHOR

One morning, while having breakfast in a diner, ROBERT ALLEY started thinking about ghosts. He wondered why everyone always assumes that ghosts are bad. "After all, there are more nice people than bad people in the world," he explains. "So why shouldn't the same be true for ghosts?"

Just then, the diner got very busy. Mr. Alley wondered what a nice ghost would do in a situation like that. And what would everyone else think about it? He grabbed a pen and a handful of napkins, and *The Ghost in Dobbs Diner* was born.

After graduating from Haverford College in Pennsylvania, Mr. Alley illustrated several books. *The Ghost in Dobbs Diner* is the first he has written and illustrated for Parents. Mr. Alley lives in Massachusetts.